JALOPY

For Elliot, Jack and Elsie

ORCHARD BOOKS
96 Leonard Street, London EC2A 4XD
Orchard Books Australia
32/45-51 Huntley Street, Alexandria, NSW 2015
ISBN 1 84362 266 1 (hardback)
ISBN 1 84362 267 X (paperback)
First published in Great Britain in 2003
First paperback publication in 2004
Text © Geraldine McCaughrean 2003
Illustrations © Ross Collins 2003
The rights of Geraldine McCaughrean to be identified as the author
and of Ross Collins to be identified as the illustrator of this
work have been asserted by them in accordance with the
Copyright, Designs and Patents Act, 1988.
A CIP catalogue record for this book is available
from the British Library.
1 3 5 7 9 10 8 6 4 2 (hardback)
1 3 5 7 9 10 8 6 4 2 (paperback)
Printed in Great Britain

JALOPY

A car's story in five drivers

GERALDINE McCAUGHREAN
Illustrated by Ross Collins

ORCHARD BOOKS

2653716

THE WINNER

Mrs Ethel Thomas had time on her hands. She even wore two watches: one pretty little gold one, and a big, heavy watch with a thick leather strap. The second had once belonged to her husband. It did not go any more, but then neither did her husband. One day, back in 1980, his heart had stopped, like the tick of a broken watch.

Mrs Thomas was lonely without

him. Sometimes she found herself talking to the radio.

"Thank you, Mr Beethoven, that was very nice." "A little quieter please, Mr Strauss."

Sometimes, in the supermarket, she spoke to the jam pots as she chose between the plum, greengage and seedless raspberry: "Now which of you is coming home to tea with me?"

But if she ever caught herself talking to herself, she stopped at once. She did not want people to think she was getting old and silly.

At the supermarket, Ethel always bought a magazine. She never knitted the pattern inside, never cooked the recipes, but she did do the competitions. Ethel had time on her hands, and to fill it, she did competitions.

One day the magazine asked her to say, in not more than 15 words, why she would like to win a car. Ethel knew just what to write. "I would like to win a car because I have never won anything ever."

It was true. At least, up until that day it was true.

Ethel Thomas won the car. And what a car it was! Red, like wartime lipstick, with soft white seats and a radio set into a wood-look dashboard.

"Well, Mrs Thomas, how do you feel about your lucky win?" said the man from the local paper.

"Perplexed," said Ethel.

Next week there was a photograph of her in the paper, standing by the car, holding up the keys.

'Lucky Winner is over the moon' said the words. (The reporter thought 'perplexed' was too hard for his readers.)

Now, Ethel had someone else to talk to: her shiny red car. The curved grille at the front looked like a big silver smile, and Ethel liked people who smiled. She called it 'Jalopy', and took to drinking her morning tea in the back. She would take a Thermos flask and sprawl on the soft, white leather, listening to the radio and pretending to be the Queen. Waving.

One day a man even waved back. He wore a bungee cord for a coat belt, a towel for a hat, newspaper shoulder-pads, and a wastepaper basket under one arm. Bending close to the window, he said, "Feet are best, of course."

"Best for what?" said Ethel, winding down the window.

"For getting about, of course! Me, I walk everywhere, me."

Ethel poured a second cup of tea, and the stranger joined her in the car. "My name's Ethel," she said. "What's yours?"

"Rover," said the man. "Red Rover."

"And where do you live, Mr Rover?"

Red Rover flung wide his arms. "Under the sky! Under the stars! I live as the birds do, I do, roaming the wide world and sleeping under the hedgerows!"

"Don't you get rather wet?"

"The rain makes me grow!" declared Red Rover flexing his muscles," and the sun makes me blossom!"

"But you have a home somewhere, surely? Everyone should have a home."

Mr Rover grew red in the face and threw the dregs of his tea out of the car window. They splashed a passing car. "And you should get a job, Ethel. Everyone should have a job!"

"I am seventy-one," said Mrs Thomas. "I don't want a job!"

"Exactly! And I am Red Rover and I do not want a home! Never talk of

'Everyone'. 'Everyone' is different!"

"You started it, with the feet!" retorted Mrs Thomas. "Feet are best, you said, when I know for a fact that some feet aren't! Some feet won't carry a person as far as the post-box without complaining!"

And that was how their friendship began. After that, the two often sat together in Jalopy and drank tea and argued. It was lovely.

Ethel's relations did not agree. When they came on their yearly visit, they fitted a burglar alarm to the house, and bolts on the garden gate. "What are you thinking of, Ethel dear?" they said. "A perfect stranger! He might be a thief - or a killer! "

Ethel only smiled.

"What a silly old woman you are becoming, Ethel dear!" they said fondly. "He probably wants your money!"

Ethel only hooted with laughter.

"And you really should rent a garage for that lovely car, Ethel. Is it insured? Oh, and by the way... when you die, can we have it?"

Ethel Thomas only sipped her tea and listened to the sound of her feet throbbing.

When winter blew in under the door, Ethel's feet throbbed even more, and she thought of Red Rover plodding along the stony lanes. When rain lashed her windows, Ethel thought of Red Rover's newspaper shoulder pads turning into papier-mache. When fog filled up the windowpanes like freezing milk, Ethel thought of Red Rover and worried. She wiped the misty window with her elbow. Beyond the garden wall, Jalopy glowed as red as a chestnut-seller's stove. "Oh thank you, Jalopy! You have given me the most wonderful idea!"

It was Christmas Eve when Red Rover next came splashing along the slushy pavement. Ethel threw open the car door and brandished a vacuum flask. There in the back seat of the shiny red motor, she took Rover's hand in hers and set before him, like a plate of biscuits, her wonderful idea.

"I want YOU to have Jalopy!" she said.

Red Rover gave such a start his tea spilled on the white leather. He pulled his hand out of hers and wrenched open the door. The bungee cord around his waist got tangled in the safety belt and twice he was pulled back into the car, but at last he broke free.

A bus had to swerve round him as he marched away down the brow of the road, shouting, and "How could you, Ethel? You of all people! Charity! The insult! You people with your flashy motors and burglar alarms! You think you are better than my kind, but I'll have you know...."

His voice tailed away. Ethel shut the car door, locked it and sat listening to the crackle of sleet and a sad song playing on the radio.

"You never gave me time to explain," she said aloud. "I can't afford to keep the car.... It's too expensive. But you! You could still travel the world! But in Jalopy you could see more of it! And then you could come back and tell me everything you've seen!" Sleet melted into tears on the widows. Ethel touched the bungee cord lying on the seat. "You didn't let me explain. I've never been anywhere. I've never seen anything. I can't drive, you see."

Lonelier than ever now, Mrs Thomas bought a cat. The cat made her sneeze, but then everyone needs some excitement in their lives, even if it is only sneezing.

THE ROBBERS

Masher saw the advertisement in the shop window. He read it out to Spug.

FREE TO A GOOD OWNER
NICE RED CAR
UNWANTED PRIZE
Apply 34 Rosemary Drive after 8am

"Go and get it, Spug," said Masher "We need a car, to do the bank job."

So Spug went round to Rosemary Drive.

Even though it was early morning, there were already several people outside the house. They had all read the advertisement.

Spug went to the front of the queue and pushed in.

"Excuse me, but I was here first!" said the first lady.

Spug bunched his fists and screwed up his eyebrows. "Scram!" he said in a voice as loud as a canon.

When Ethel opened the door, there was no one there but a big rhinoceros of a man in scaly brown leather and football boots.

"I've come for the car," said Spug.

"I'll get you the keys," said Ethel. She went indoors again. He could hear her sneezing her way around the house, looking for the keys.

Quick as a wink, Spug seized his chance. He leapt the garden wall, smashed a window and climbed inside the car. Pulling loose some wires, he somehow started up the engine. Then he drove off at high speed.

Ethel Thomas watched him go, from her front door. The keys dangled from her finger. "What a strange young man," she said to the cat, and sneezed again.

"I stole it while her back was turned!" declared Smug proudly.

"But she was going to give it to you for free," said Masher, noting the broken window. "Spug, you are a fool."

Masher told Spug to paint Jalopy black. "Nobody notices a black car. We will glide up to the bank like an evening shadow and slip away again like... er... er..."

"Another shadow?" said Spug

"Exactly!"

But as they drove into town, it began to rain. Big red spots appeared on Jalopy's black bonnet. "Oo look! The car's got measles," said Spug. "No wonder that woman gave it away."

"What paint did you use?" asked Masher.

"That stuff I stole from school," said Spug.

"Spug you are an idiot," said Masher.

Soon all the poster paint washed off Jalopy and she was red again - as red as Superman's cape - when she stopped outside the Easy-Bank. People turned to admire the shiny red car, the smiling silver grille.

Masher and Spug had not been bank robbers for very long – only for one day, in fact. The lady at the Job Centre told them they could not be astronauts because they had not passed any exams. She said they should try gardening or selling hamburgers. But Masher made up his mind then and there. If they could not be astronauts, they would be bank robbers instead.

21

Outside, on the pavement, Spug asked, "Is it hard? Can anyone do it?"

Masher went back into the Job Centre. "Do you need exams to be a bank robber?"

"No," said the lady, "only to be a bank manager," and Masher said thank you very much.

So here they were, outside the Easy-Bank. They put on their swimming goggles, took hold of their snorkels like guns, and walked into the bank. (They had seen gangsters on TV, so they knew how to walk.)

The bank was full of people, but only one till was open. It was lunchtime. All the bank clerks but one were out at lunch. Spug went to the front of the queue.

"Wait your turn!" complained the queue.

Seeing their swimming goggles,

though, the clerk behind the window said, "Ah! Have you come to clean out our fish? Follow me."

She took them to the Bank Manager's office. (The Manager was out at lunch.) and showed them a big tank full of goldfish. Spug was delighted. "Look at all the pretty fish, Masher!"

"I am going to lunch now, said the clerk. "When you have finished, just let yourselves out."

When she was gone, they went through to the tills and took out all the money. They were behind the counter now, so customers tapped on the glass screen. "Can you please serve us!" they said.

Masher and Spug shook their heads. "We don't have the right exams," they said, loading the money into their swimming bags.

Spug wanted to take some of the

goldfish, too, but Masher told him he could go to a pet shop later and buy a whole tankful.

Outside in the car, they did not stop to count their stolen money. (Counting in tens and fives is a bit difficult and it takes time.) They simply hid the money under the white leather seats and drove away.

"Can we go to the pet shop now?" said Spug as Jalopy purred along.

"First I think we should rob another bank," said Masher. "It's so easy."

So they parked Jalopy – as red and shiny as Spiderman's legs – right outside the SuperSafe Bank. Many heads turned to admire the sleek motorcar with its spokey wheels.

Traffic Warden Iona Clamp also turned her head. Iona Clamp clicked her tongue and the button on her ballpoint pen. Her sharp little fingers clicked the keys of her mobile 'phone, too, as she called for... The Collector .

No one messes with The Collector.

Its twin forks scooped up shiny red Jalopy and carried her away. Iona Clamp smiled grimly. No one parked on yellow lines when she was in town.

Two minutes later, Masher and Spug ran out of the bank, chased by ten security guards, two big dogs, four workmen with sledgehammers, an off-duty policeman and the clang of alarm bells.

"Quick! Into the car!" cried Masher.

"What car?" said Spug.

They looked right. They looked left. But Jalopy was gone.

Heavy hands fell on their shoulders. Dogs snapped at their heels. But Masher and Spug just stood scouring the street for their getaway car.

They were ... how shall I put it? ... perplexed.

Masher and Spug were in prison for some time. Jalopy stood unclaimed in the Police Pound. Because she had no number plates, the Police could not trace her real owner. And so she stood – through spring rain and summer's heat – a car as red as a traffic light saying: 'Stop'.

THE BEST DRIVER
ON THE ROAD

Alfred Gippy had driving gloves and he knew how to use them. Ever since driving his first pedal car among the table legs, at the age of two, Gippy had known he was the best driver on the road.

"If only everyone drove as well as I do," Gippy complained.

Gippy hated other drivers. They took the spaces he wanted in car parks.

They got in his way when he wanted to drive fast. Some of them had bigger cars than his, which was plainly unfair.

"Idiots! Nincompoops! Wimps!" snarled Gippy. "Shouldn't be allowed!"

Gippy hated pedestrians, too. They used zebra crossings just to spite him. They stepped off the kerb with their guide dogs. They even had streets in Town where only they could walk.

"Pests! Nuisances! A menace!" hissed Gippy. "Shouldn't be allowed!"

Worst of all, Gippy hated signs telling him what to do. If a sign said 'Slow', he always went faster. If a sign said 'No Entry', he turned in. If a sign said 'One Way', Gippy drove in both directions. NO PARKING said the notice outside the corner shop, so Gippy always parked there when he bought his cigarettes.

One day he came out to find The Collector scooping up his car, while Traffic Warden Iona Clamp looked on.

Gippy broke her pencil across his knee. "You people don't understand: a good driver can park safely anywhere!" But it made no difference. He still had to go to the Police Pound and pay a fine to get back his car.

That was when he saw Jalopy – as red as temper and wearing no number plates. She was twice as powerful as his own car. She was the same zingy colour as the pedal car he had had when he was two. And there she stood, just gathering dust, just rusting away, just bursting to be driven by a man like Gippy.

It was the work of moments to take the number plates off his own car and fix them to Jalopy. Then Gippy drove home telling himself, "People don't understand: a good car needs a good driver."

Jalopy had a few patches of rust, but her engine was as good as new. Gippy could drive her so fast that his children were sick on the back seat and his wife begged, "Remember the Speed Limit!"

"You people don't understand," said Gippy. "Speed limits were only invented for bad drivers. A good driver can go as fast as his car lets him."

Jalopy let Gippy go very fast indeed, dodging from lane to lane to nip past slower cars.

Nippy Mr Gippy.

When he found a stretch of open road, he drove so fast that his children in the back seat screamed and his wife burst into tears beside him. With a cigarette clenched between his teeth and the steering wheel gripped in both fists, Alfred Gippy knew he was the best driver ever to zip along a road.

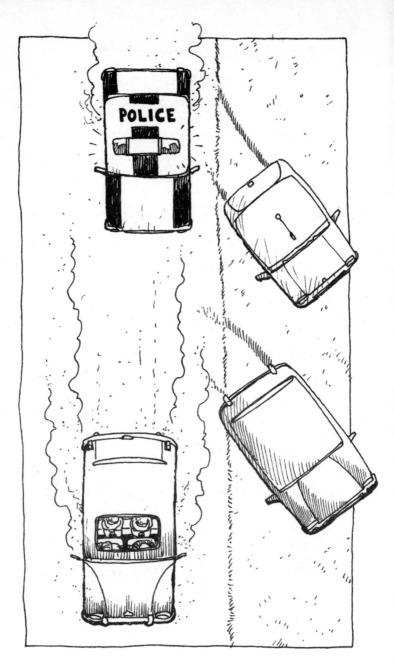

Zippy Mr Gippy.

When another driver annoyed him, he used his clever driving to teach them a lesson. He would drive by, very close, and clip the wing mirror of the other car, so that it fell off with a tinkling of glass. Wonderful noise. Clip. Tinkle.

Clippy Mr Gippy.

When the police sirens wailed behind him and police lights blinked in his rear-view mirror, Gippy said, "I wonder who they are chasing? Some bad driver, I suppose. There are so many of them about."

"You will lose your driving licence for five years, Mr Gippy..." said the Judge.

Alfred Gippy shook his head. He could hardly believe how unfairly he was being treated! "You people don't understand: these stupid Laws weren't made for good drivers. And I'm a good driver, I am!"

"...And you will pay a fine of one thousand pounds," said the Judge.

Lippy Mr Gippy.

Alfred Gippy was horrified. For five whole years, he must not drive!

Not drive? It was like telling a dancer not to dance or a singer not to sing! Here he was – the best driver on the road – and he was forbidden to take his motor out of the garage or wear his string-backed driving gloves. He went down to the pub and poured out his sad, sad story to the barman.

"You should go down the Race Track like me," said the barman. "A race track isn't a road. Anyone can drive down the Race Track, licence or no licence."

Of course! Why had Gippy not thought of it before? He would be a racing driver! His Destiny was staring him in the face! When people saw his skill, they would beg him to drive for their team. He would race in Brazil and Monte Carlo, at Silverstone and Indianapolis!

Happy Mr Gippy.

Next day Gippy told his wife to drive him to the RaceTrack. The children went too. (Gippy wanted them to see him win his first race.) His spirits soared when he saw the other cars lined up on the starting grid. They were all dirty and dented, doors tied shut with string, no glass in the windows. "Plainly terrible drivers," Gippy told his family.

"Er...Dad..." said his son.

But Gippy was in no mood for chatter. "Get out, now, and watch a master at work!"

Jalopy simmered on the starting grid. A klaxon blew. They were off! With a cigarette between his lips and the wheel between his fists, Gippy roared away down the track: best driver on the road. Ha ha ha!

Then he bit though his cigarette as the car behind crashed into his bumper.

Another car crunched in from the right.

Another barged him from the left. Gippy cursed. "Idiots! Nincompoops! Fools!"

Like a bunch of big bullies the other cars shunted and shoved Jalopy. They pushed her up against the metal barrier. They bounced her off the piles of tyres. They pushed her along like a supermarket trolley. They crumpled her like an old, Coca-Cola can.

In his hurry to show the world his genius, Gippy had missed seeing the banner at the entrance of the RaceTrack:

TONITE
STOCK CAR RACING

"Stop! That's not fair! Don't! That's dangerous! Stop it! That's against the Rules!" screamed Gippy as the other cars bumped and biffed him. But there are no rules in Stock Car racing. The idea is just to bang about until every other car on the track has lost the fight.

Soon every stock car in the race was streaked with Jalopy's red paint. Her white leather seats were sprinkled with broken glass. Her wing mirrors were gone. Her bonnet flapped loose. She had been squeezed and stretched like an accordion, and her exhaust pipe was dragging along the ground.

As for Gippy, his hair was as white as his seat; his fingers poked through his string-backed gloves and he had swallowed his cigarette. Then and there he swore he would never again sit behind a steering wheel – no, not if his life depended on it. He asked his wife to telephone for a tow truck.

"If I hitch up the exhaust pipe with this bungee cord, dear, I might be able to drive," said his wife helpfully.

"I'd sooner walk," said Gippy. "I'm feeling rather sick."

Jippy Mr Gippy.

THE LEARNER
DRIVER

Tyrone really wanted a bike. All his friends had bikes. But his father wanted him to have the best. He always did. So he bought Tyrone a car.

If he really had to drive, Tyrone wanted a small car. He had only just passed his Driving Test. Small cars were easier to park and to turn round. But his father wanted him to have the best, so he bought Tyrone a great big car: found it in the local paper.

BIG RED CAR
Must be seen
to be believed.
01770 9872345 (Gippy)

"Big cars are safer than small cars if you have an accident," said Tyrone's father.

"Staying home is even safer," thought Tyrone, but he did not say so.

The man selling the car had white hair and a wild look in his eyes. "Good as new, good as new," he kept saying. His hands were stained with bright red paint, so that he looked as if he had just murdered someone.

The car was beautiful. Tyrone had to admit that much. It had white leather seats and a silver grille like a big, silly grin.

"Good as new, good as new!" Mr Gippy repeated.

"What are you waiting for, son?" said her father. "Take it for a drive while I write out the cheque."

So Tyrone went for a drive in Jalopy. He chose only the widest, quietest roads. Even so, he felt like an ant paddling a canoe along the Amazon River. He did not want to park or turn round or go to right or left, and so he drove on and on in a straight line. In fact Tyrone drove on right through town.

He passed Masher and Spug as they stood at a bus stop, on their way home from prison.

"Did you see that?" said Masher.

"That was our car!" said Spug. "The one with our money in!" And they set off to run after it. When they could not keep up, they stole a motorbike-and-side-car and began to chase the big red car. With luck, the money stolen from

EasyBank still lay hidden under its white leather seats!

Tyrone looked in his driving mirror and saw them coming up behind. Soon they were almost nudging his back bumper. Two angry faces peered in through his back window. The driver was shaking his fist, and the passenger was shouting.

"What have I done wrong now?" thought Tyrone and went a little faster.

With a roar like a lion, the motorbike-and-sidecar caught up, pulled out and began to pass him. The driver was pulling faces and the passenger was shouting, "Stop, you! Give us the money!" It put Tyrone in mind of highwaymen. He bit his lip and pressed down on the pedal for more speed.

Horn honking, the motorbike and sidecar tried to pull in front of the big

red car. Tyrone stopped caring what he had done wrong, and pushed his foot down to the floor. Away roared Jalopy – down a hill and over a level crossing: rattle, clatter, boompf!

That was when the bungee cord broke.

Alfred Gippy had mended the broken catch on the bonnet using a bungee cord he found in the car. Now it broke, the bonnet flew up and Tyrone thought he was seeing the End of the World through the windscreen: red and fiery and very, very close.

He certainly could not see anything else.

Blinded by the shiny red bonnet, he could not see the road ahead, could not see the fork in the road ahead either. When the road forked to right and left, Tyrone drove straight ahead.

Jalopy left the road, crashed

through a fence, and landed nose-down in a ditch, with a noise like a flying cow coming in to land.

Masher stopped the motorbike.

"Oooer," said Spug.

They sidled over to the hole in the fence. Only the back wheels of the big car stuck out of the ditch, and thin wisps of smoke rose from the wreckage.

"Should we climb down and look for our money?" said Spug.

"You are an idiot, Spug," said Masher. "Call the Fire Brigade. Then let's get out of here!"

When the Fire Brigade came, it was led by Station Officer Bold. Bravely she squirted the smoking car. Courageously she clambered down into the ditch. Expertly she prised open the buckled door of the motor car. "Don't worry, sir! Soon have you out of there!"

But when Station Officer Bold saw the driver's face, her axe fell from her trembling hand. Her legs quaked inside her boots. Her heart thudded behind her medal ribbons. In all her days as a fire fighter, she had never rescued such a handsome driver.

When Tyrone looked up and saw Station Officer Bold, his blue eyes grew wider. He stopped struggling with the safety belt. He forgot the pain in his cut head. In all his timid, stay-at-home, push-biking days, Tyrone had never seen such a lovely and daring heroine.

The accident was forgotten. A
heavy, bitter rain began to fall, but it
might have been summer. Station
Officer Bold, wrapping Tyrone in her
fire-service tunic, carried him back to
the fire engine.

Though the Fire Brigade sent a
break-down lorry to pull Jalopy out of
the ditch, the lorry could not find it in
the teeming rain.

Days of rain followed, and the ditches and rivers everywhere overflowed. Floods washed away all trace of the crash. In just the same way, Love washed away all but Marriage from the minds of Tyrone and Station Officer Bold.

As Jalopy lay in the ditch, the floodwaters flowed through her from nose to tail. Then tall autumn grasses grew around and over her. Like a hibernating hedgehog she lay cocooned in brown-and-greenery.

ROVER'S RETURN

One year makes hardly any difference to a man's age. One winter can make him suddenly old. What with the floods, and the Big Freeze and the flu' epidemic, that particular winter weighed on Red Rover like a snowdrift. The open road stopped looking like a plush carpet unrolled at his feet. Now it was a gangplank jutting out over sharky waters. After all, what did the future hold in store for an ageing traveller? Once he had enjoyed sleeping out under the stars. Now the stars overhung him like the points of a million daggers waiting to drop on his head.

So he was glad when he stumbled across a rusty old car lying in a roadside ditch. It was sunk up to its roof in dead grass and nettles. Only a few spots of paintwork still showed, red and rusty, like the spotty tops of toadstools. From the tip of the buckled bonnet dangled a soggy bungee cord. Red was grateful enough to fasten it round his flapping coat in place of the one he had lost.

Climbing inside through the sunroof, Red Rover closed it behind him and curled up on the back seat. It was damp and mouldy, with rat droppings on the dashboard and snails on the windows. But to a man with a runny nose and an aching heart it was a haven of peace. It reminded him of Ethel and her cosy red Jalopy, of tea and biscuits and the car radio playing.

Next morning, grey light showered in through the frozen sunroof. Red Rover lay on his spongy bed and thought about Life. His feet no longer itched to tramp the lanes and highways in fact his feet said, "We want to stay home today. We deserve a rest."

For a long time Red lay watching the snails ice skating upside down on the frozen sunroof. Even in this cosy nest his breath made white clouds in the air.

"Well. Best be off," said Red, bravely struggling to stand up.

"Why?" said his feet. Like a pair of mutineers, they deserted him and slid away down the back of the slippery seat. And there they stuck.

Half out of the sunroof, feet wedged, Red tugged and heaved with all his might but all that happened was that his boots came off. There was nothing for it but to wriggle back inside and prise off the back seat.

There lay his mutinous boots. They were afloat in a sea of green and blue bank notes. Red Rover was rich.

Red and his feet decided, then and there, to buy a house. Boots-in-hand, he squirmed out of the car and danced into town, feverish with flu and quite dizzy with joy. A house, yes! With warm fireplaces and dry beds, deep soft carpets and a kitchen stove! 'For Sale' notices wagged at him in the wind, like railway signals standing at green.

"Pick a home – any home! – and settle down!" begged his weary feet, although somehow they managed to dance with joy at the end of his weary legs.

Red Rover turned in at the very next 'For Sale' sign and knocked on the door. "Good morning! Please may I buy your house?"

"Red!" said Ethel.

"Ethel?" said Red.

If she had not spoken his name, he

would never have known her. Her face was pale and thin, with big black circles around her eyes and a sore, red nose dripping.

"Atchoo," said Ethel.

"Bless you," said Red. "Bless you, bless you, bless you!"

Over a cup of tea, they told each other how kind and unkind the past year had been. Red told how his feet were no longer willing to walk the world, but how, with his new-found fortune, he could now afford a home.

"Shouldn't you give it back?" said Ethel. "It must belong to somebody."

"How could I possibly find out who hid it there?" asked Red, and she had to agree he was right.

Ethel mopped her nose and introduced the cat. "I feel too ill and too old now, to live here alone."

"You aren't suffering from old age!"

exclaimed Red. "You are just allergic to the cat! Leave this to me!"

And he built a Cat Palace at the end of the garden, using pieces of scrap from the wrecked car nearby. The Palace had mossy leather seats and chrome door handles, a silver grille for a drawbridge and even a working radio.

With the cat out-of-doors, Ethel stopped sneezing. So there was no need to sell the house after all. But then there was no need for Red to buy one either. With his thousands, he bought a big, flashy motorhome and parked it in front of Ethel's house.

After the wedding – and every summer after that - Red and Ethel drove off together in their motorhome, to see the world.

The cat did not mind at all.

And neither did Jalopy, resting her bare bones in a cradle of green grass and scarlet elderberries.

The Relations did not like it, though: no, not one bit.